Farmer Claude
and
Farmer Maude's

Editor: Jill Kalz

Page Production: Tracy Kaehler

Creative Director: Keith Griffin

Editorial Director: Carol Jones

First American edition published in 2006 by

Picture Window Books

5115 Excelsior Boulevard

Suite 232

Minneapolis, MN 55416

877-845-8392

www.picturewindowbooks.com

First published in Australia by

Ice Water Press

An imprint of @Source Pty Limited

Unit 3, Level 1, 114 Old Pittwater Road

Brookvale NSW 2100 Australia

Ph: 61 2 9939 8222; Fax: 61 2 99398666

Email: sales@sourceoz.com

Copyright © 2004 by Ice Water Press

Printed in the United States of America.

Library of Congress Cataloging-in-Publication Data
Scott, Janine.
The rowdy rooster / by Janine Scott ; illustrated by Ian Forss.
p. cm. — (Farmer Claude and Farmer Maude)
Summary: Two tired farmers and a shed full of grumpy animals have had
enough of the rooster waking them at five o'clock each morning, but Farmer
Maude has a plan to help the rooster sleep in.
ISBN 1-4048-1699-2 (hardcover)
[1. Sleep—Fiction. 2. Roosters—Fiction. 3. Farmers—Fiction. 4. Domestic
animals—Fiction. 5. Stories in rhyme.] I. Forss, Ian, ill. II. Title.
PZ8.3.S4275Row 2005
[E]—dc22   2005029470

Farmer Claude and Farmer Maude

The Rowdy Rooster

by Janine Scott

illustrated by Ian Forss

PiCTURE WiNDOW BOOKS
Minneapolis, Minnesota

Farmer Claude and Farmer Maude
were asleep on a Sunday morning.
The sheep, the dog, the goat, and the hog
all woke up without warning.

A rooster is a male
chicken that is more
than 1 year old.

The rowdy rooster crowed out loud,
just as the day was dawning.
It was such a shock, at 5 o'clock—
too early in the morning!

He woke up the sheep.
He woke up the dog.
He woke up the goat.
He woke up the hog.

"I need my sleep," bleated the sheep,
and the dog just barked where he lay.
The goat stamped his feet and bared his teeth,
and the hog shook his head in dismay.

Roosters cannot crow
unless they stretch
out their necks.

Farmer Claude and Farmer Maude
woke up with a shock.

Farmer Maude checked the time and cried, "It's 5 o'clock!"

"What should we do?"
cried Farmer Claude.

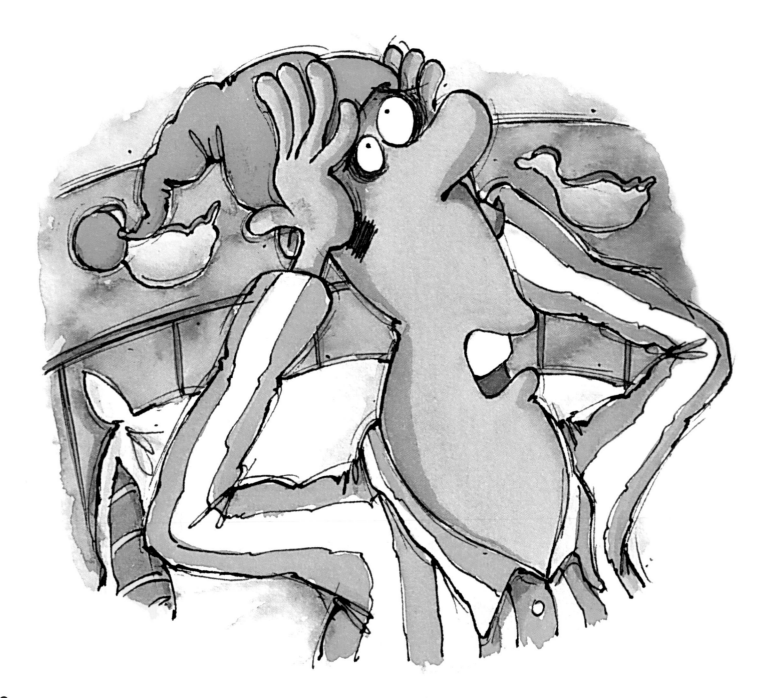

"I have a plan!"
cried Farmer Maude.

So Farmer Claude and Farmer Maude walked to the big red shed.

The sheep, the dog, the goat, and the hog
followed where they led.

"Look at that bed!" the farmers said.
"There are chunks of straw.
There are chunks of sticks.
There are chunks of wood.
There are chunks of bricks!"

"No wonder the rooster doesn't sleep,"
baaed the tired sheep.
The dog just yawned, the goat bared his teeth,
and the hog fell down in a heap.

Dried stalks of wheat or other grains are called straw. Most farm animals sleep on straw beds.

"It's time for your plan!"
cried Farmer Claude.

"It's shearing time!"
cried Farmer Maude.

So Farmer Claude and Farmer Maude
got scissors from out of the shed.
With a snip and a snap and a snippety-snap,
they were making that rooster a bed.

They sheared the sheep.

They clipped the dog.

They plucked the goat.

They snipped the hog.

An average sheep can produce about 10 pounds (4.5 kilograms) of wool in a single shearing.

Farmer Claude and Farmer Maude
made that rooster a bed.
"This will keep our rooster asleep.
It's warm and cuddly," they said.

The very next morning, as day was dawning,
the farmers woke with a shock.
"Tick-tock, tick-tock!" said the farmhouse clock.
It was nearly 5 o'clock!

Farmer Claude and Farmer Maude
walked to the big red shed.
There inside the rooster snored,
still sleeping on his bed.

Dogs sleep an average of 15 hours a day.

"**Zzz-zz**," snored the sheep.

"**Zzz-zz**," snored the dog.

"**Zzz-zz**," snored the goat.

"**Zzz-zz**," snored the hog.

Zzz-zz

Zzz-zz

Zzz-zz

Zzz-zz

Farmer Claude and Farmer Maude
watched them sleeping, too.
Then Farmer Claude and Farmer Maude
crowed, "COCK-A-DOODLE-DOO!"

1. What time did the rowdy rooster crow?

2. Name the four animals the rooster woke up.

Rooster's Recap

3. What was the rooster's old bed made of?

4. What did Farmer Claude and Farmer Maude use to shear the animals?

5. Why did Farmer Claude and Farmer Maude shear the sheep, clip the dog, pluck the goat, and snip the hog?

6. What did Farmer Claude and Farmer Maude say when they saw the snoring animals?

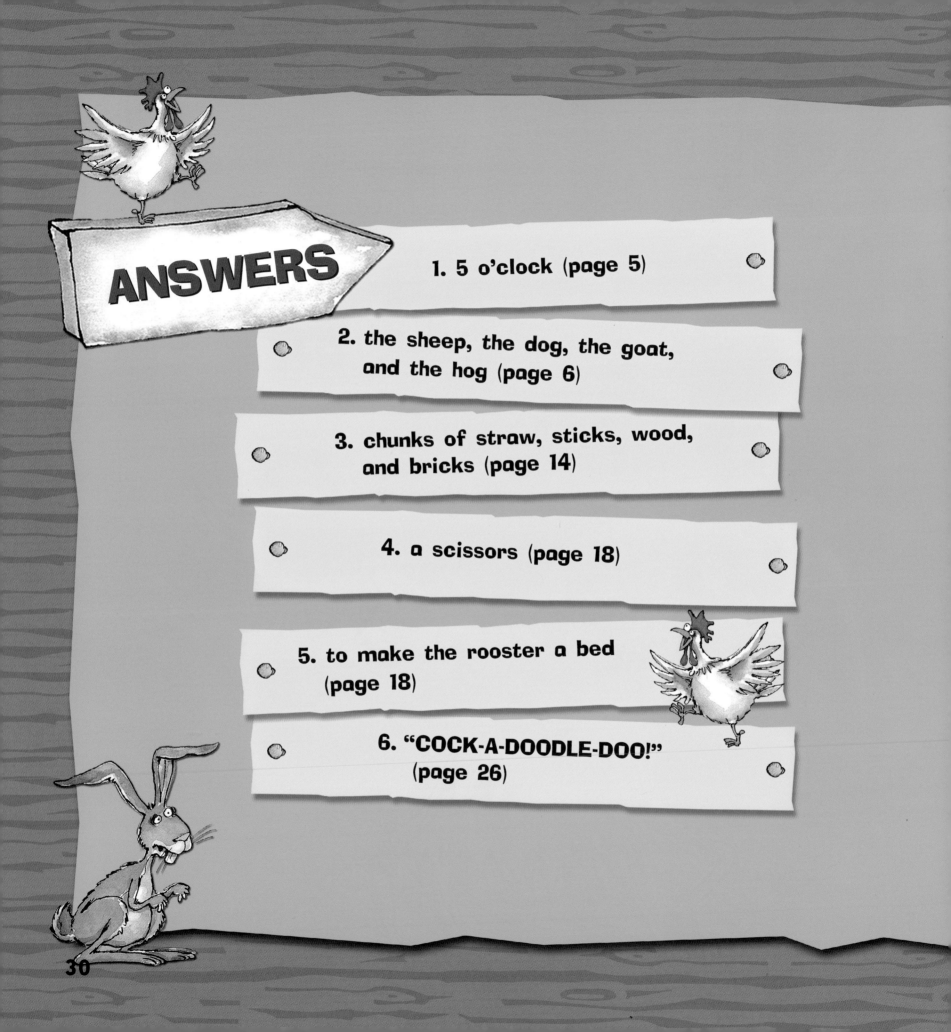

ANSWERS

1. 5 o'clock (page 5)

2. the sheep, the dog, the goat, and the hog (page 6)

3. chunks of straw, sticks, wood, and bricks (page 14)

4. a scissors (page 18)

5. to make the rooster a bed (page 18)

6. "COCK-A-DOODLE-DOO!" (page 26)

30

To Learn More

On the Web

FactHound offers a safe, fun way to find Internet sites related to this book. All of the sites on FactHound have been researched by our staff.

1. Visit *www.facthound.com*
2. Type in this special code for age-appropriate sites: 1404816992
3. Click on the FETCH IT button.

Your trusty FactHound will fetch the best sites for you!

At the Library

DK Publishing. *Farm Animals*. New York: DK Publishing, 2004.

Kutner, Merrily. *Down on the Farm*. New York: Holiday House, 2004.

Rostoker-Gruber, Karen. *Rooster Can't Cock-a-Doodle-Doo*. New York: Dial Books, 2004.

Wolfman, Judy. *Life on a Dairy Farm*. Minneapolis: Carolrhoda Books, 2004.

READY FOR MORE ADVENTURES?

Charming and funny, Farmer Claude and Farmer Maude are anything but boring. Full of great ideas and in love with adventure, these odd farmers know how to have a good time wherever they are!

Farmer Claude

Farmer Maude

Hog

Goat

Dog

Sheep

Rooster

What a group of unlucky characters! Storm clouds follow them, rain soaks their beds, and the farmers wake them at the crack of dawn. But the animals make it through together—and even share a smile or two.

Look for All of the Books in the Farmer Claude and Farmer Maude Series: